This Book Is
My Best Friend

For all the books that are my friends,
and all the friends I made through books
—R. R.

SIMON & SCHUSTER BOOKS FOR YOUNG READERS
An imprint of Simon & Schuster Children's Publishing Division
1230 Avenue of the Americas, New York, New York 10020
© 2023 by Robin Robinson
Book design by Krista Vossen © 2023 by Simon & Schuster, Inc.
All rights reserved, including the right of reproduction in whole or in part in any form.
SIMON & SCHUSTER BOOKS FOR YOUNG READERS and related marks are trademarks
of Simon & Schuster, Inc.
For information about special discounts for bulk purchases, please contact
Simon & Schuster Special Sales at 1-866-506-1949 or business@simonandschuster.com.
The Simon & Schuster Speakers Bureau can bring authors to your live event. For more
information or to book an event, contact the Simon & Schuster Speakers Bureau at
1-866-248-3049 or visit our website at www.simonspeakers.com.
The text for this book was set in Else and Atkinson Hyperlegible.
The illustrations for this book were rendered digitally.
Manufactured in China
0922 SCP
First Edition
2 4 6 8 10 9 7 5 3 1
CIP data for this book is available from the Library of Congress.
ISBN 9781665906814
ISBN 9781665906821 (ebook)

This Book Is My Best Friend

FACTORY FRIENDS

ROBIN ROBINSON

Simon & Schuster Books for Young Readers
New York London Toronto Sydney New Delhi

You don't understand. This book is my BEST FRIEND.

I love this book to the very last word, which is "mouse," my favorite animal.

Sometimes I like to pretend to be a mouse while I read this book.

I see. But there's
only one book.

And there are
two of us.

Well, how about this book?
You can build yourself a
whole new robot friend!

What about a book with ALL the other kinds of mice to keep you company?